DISNEY'S

My Very First Winnie the Pooh™

Sweet Dreams, Pooh

Kathleen W. Zoehfeld   Illustrated by Robbin Cuddy

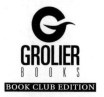

GROLIER
BOOKS

BOOK CLUB EDITION

Based on the Pooh stories by A. A. Milne
(copyright The Pooh Properties Trust).

Printed in the United States of America.

First published by Disney Press, New York, NY
This edition published by Grolier Books, ISBN: 0-7172-8866-8
Grolier Books is a division of Grolier Enterprises, Inc.

Winnie the Pooh stood back and admired his work. "Ten new pots of honey," he sighed happily.

"Very nice," said Tigger. "Just make sure that horrible heffalump doesn't eat them tonight."

"The herrable hoffalump!?" asked Pooh.

"He's a greedy gobbler!" said Tigger.

"You've seen him?" asked Pooh.

"No," said Tigger, "but it's even worse when you don't see him. You can't be too careful when a heffalump's sneaking around."

"I'll be careful," said Pooh.

"Worraworrow," growled Tigger bravely. "T-T-F-N—ta-ta for now!"

"Good night, Tigger."

Pooh locked his door. His house seemed big and empty.

He climbed in bed and pulled his quilt up over his nose. And he stayed that way for a long time.

"Hurrible Hoffalump," he thought. "Must keep watch. . . ." He watched and he watched and he watched, until he couldn't keep his eyes open any longer. . . .

Then, suddenly, his house shook like thunder.
A big red heffalump crashed through the door.
He broke dishes and toppled the lamps. He
stomped to Pooh's cupboard and guzzled up
three pots of honey.

"Oh!" cried Pooh.

The heffalump turned and looked at Pooh with his horrible green eyes. He snuffled him

with his long blue snout.

"Ho-ho!" he said. "Now I'm going to eat you!"

The heffalump scrunched a honeypot down over Pooh's head.

"Mmppfh!" cried Pooh.

He jumped out of bed.

He reached up to pull the pot off his head, but . . . the pot was gone! The heffalump was gone, too.

"Where is he hiding?" Pooh wondered. He was afraid to look. He ran to Piglet's house as fast as he could.

"Help! Help! A ho-horrible heffalump is ha-hiding in my huh-house," puffed Pooh.

"A huh? A heff? A who?" asked Piglet, rubbing his eyes.

"A heffalump. Hurry!"

Piglet had no time to think. If he had had time to think, he certainly would not be rushing out in the night to help Pooh find a horrible heffalump.

"Come out, heffalump!" cried Pooh.

Piglet grabbed Pooh's broom and held it high over his head.

"Pooh?" asked Piglet, who had finally had time to think. "What will we do with the heffalump when we find him?"

Pooh thought and thought and thought.

"Maybe we should go get Christopher Robin," suggested Piglet.

"Good thinking," said Pooh.

Christopher Robin was in bed when they arrived. "Poor Pooh," he said, "you must have had a bad dream. Heffalumps aren't real."

"He was real," said Pooh. "I felt him snuffle me with his blue snout. He said he was going to eat me!"

"If there is a heffalump in your house, then Piglet and I will help you find him," said Christopher Robin stoutly.

"We will? I-I mean, yes, we will," said Piglet.

Together they mounted an expedition to find the horrible heffalump and chase him from Pooh's house forever.

They looked under Pooh's bed.

They looked behind his mirror.

They lifted the tablecloth and peered under the table.

They opened his cupboard. All ten pots stood side by side, just as Pooh had left them.

Pooh scratched behind his ear. "It must have been a dream. But why did it seem so real?"

"Dreams can seem real," said Christopher Robin. "But they happen only in your mind."

"Oh," said Pooh, "but if I was asleep, how could my mind be making up a heffalump?"

"Every night, when your body sleeps, your brain stays awake part of the time," said Christopher Robin.

"That's when you're dreaming!" cried Piglet.

"Right!" said Christopher Robin. "Usually dreams are nice—or they're just boring, and you forget them as soon as you wake up. But if you're especially tired or worried about something, then sometimes a dream turns into a bad dream, or nightmare."

"I was a little worried," said Pooh, thinking of what Tigger had said. "And I'm so sleepy. But . . ."

Piglet tucked Pooh in bed.

". . . what if my brain brings the heffalump back?" asked Pooh.

"It's your dream," said Christopher Robin. "You're in charge. If he comes back, just look him in the eye and say: 'Heffalump—go away!'"

"Heffalump go away . . . Heffalump go away . . . Heff . . . go . . . ," Pooh repeated, until at last he was fast asleep again.

Piglet and Christopher Robin tiptoed out.

Then, suddenly, Pooh's house shook like thunder. A big red heffalump stomped right up to Pooh's bed! "Ho-ho!" he boomed.

"Hoffalump, ga-wah . . . H-Hurrfa lumph hahh!" tried Pooh. This muddled the heffalump.

"What?" he asked.

"Go away," said Pooh huskily.

The heffalump stopped. His lip began to
tremble. Tears came to his eyes.

"What's wrong?" asked Pooh.

"I just wanted a little snack, that's all," said
the heffalump, "and now, *sniff*, you're sending
me away?"

Pooh began to feel sorry he
had been so rough with the
heffalump. "I'm feeling a
bit rumbly in my
tumbly, too," he
said. "Would you
like to share a pot
of honey?"

The big heffalump looked rather silly sitting in Pooh's little chair. But he didn't seem to mind. This time, Pooh and the heffalump dreamed a sweet dream together.